HIGH WIND
FOR KANSAS

ILLUSTRATED BY W. T. MARS

HIGH WIND FOR KANSAS

MARY CALHOUN

WILLIAM MORROW & COMPANY   NEW YORK 1965

Several men in the history of America's western migration built windwagons. This story is based in part on an incident in Westport, Missouri, involving a man called Windwagon Thomas. Accounts of the event are given in *The Heritage of Kansas,* edited by Everett Rich, published by University of Lawrence Press; the *Colorado Magazine,* Jan., 1935; and the *Missouri Historical Review,* April, 1931, account by John W. Parker, reprinted from the *Kansas City Journal-Post* issue of Jan. 4, 1931. Names of characters have been changed, dialogue and incidents have been invented. My version of the story is fictional.

Mary Calhoun

Rangely, Colorado, 1964

High wind? Blow? Say, you don't know wind till you've felt the wind out west. Why, that western wind will peel off a section of the prairie—creek bed, cottonwoods, and all—and sail it away.

Out on the plains it's wide-open country, nothing to slow up Old Man Wind. He gets a running start and works himself up until

the whole countryside leans the way he's going. Just when you think the year's supply of wind has blown by today, taking the fence and your yellow hound dog, and there's a quietness and you say, "There!

8

That's all!'' here comes the wind back again. Now it's heading in the other direction, bringing along your neighbor's brick silo and old Widow Tudmore's prize rooster, a-flinging along on the breeze.

9

Well sir, there was one man who didn't just sit there hanging onto his whiskers. Once there was a man who harnessed that western wind. And this is how it happened.

One breezy morning back in 1853, the fellows were sitting in front of the livery stable in Westport, Missouri, waiting for the next excitement. Westport was a busy little town in those days, for it lay on the western edge of Missouri. It was the jumping-off

spot, the place where all those westering strangers came to outfit their wagons to take off for the gold fields and the new lands. Every few days a regular bustle of folks going through stirred up the town.

Suddenly Doc Taylor sat up like the devil
had tapped him.

"Great shakes of a horsetail! What's that coming down the street?"

Whatever it was, it came scooting along in a cloud of dust, scattering chickens and trailing dogs at full yap. Out of the dust loomed —couldn't be, sure 'twas—a sail. A boat! A boat coming down the main street of Westport, Missouri!

13

The men ran out. The thing slowed to a stop. The dust died down. And there stood the strangest contraption Westport had laid eyes on yet.

It was a wagon with a sail. A real, for-sure prairie schooner. Not a covered wagon, but a wagon bed with a post up front for a mast

and a sail rigged on it. No horses, no oxen to pull. No sir. That wagon had sailed down the street on the wind.

And in the wagon, hand on a rudder-thing at the back was a man. He was a short, wide man, bald on top, with a thick brown beard big as half of him.

Ben Purdy, the wagonmaker, swallowed his cud and yelled, "Hey, sailor, what you got there?"

A voice rumbled up out of the brown

beard. "What I have here, gentlemen, is the answer to the western migration. What I have here is—" the man waved his arm grandly "—a windwagon."

"Ho ho *he-e-e!*" the men roared. Why, this was the best fun they'd had in days.

The wagon fellow laughed along with them. But then he said, "You boys seen her move."

That's right, they had. The men quieted down and started walking around the contraption, looking her over. A sudden gust of wind made the wagon jump forward, so the bearded man furled the sail. He jumped down and trotted alongside the men, around the wagon, telling them all about it.

"My name's Jones, and I made this thing," he said. "See, I steer with the tongue."

17

Sure enough, the wagon tongue was indeed
cocked up to serve as tiller and rudder, all
wrapped up in one. The men saw now that
the wagon had come whooping down the
street backwards. The tailgate was the bow
of this land boat, and the wagon tongue was
at the stern.

"And I catch the wind like this." Jones showed them the lever that changed the set of the sail. When he wanted to stop his "ship," he just took in sail and threw out a sandbag.

Somebody's bonnet kited by. The wind was setting up for its day's fun of blowing away every loose piece of Westport. The men took shelter in the livery stable where they could talk, though Mr. Jones did most of the talking. He was a pretty big wind himself, when it came to talking.

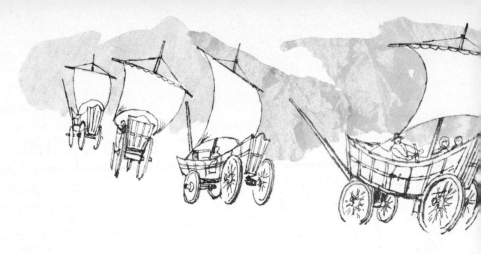

"Gentlemen, what have you got the most of? Wind. There it goes, just whistling by, not doing nobody a lick of good. Now, nothing's got a right to flourish itself around, not doing an honest day's work. Men, I propose to harness that wind!"

He explained his plan. He wanted to build a whole fleet of windwagons. He'd revolutionize the western migration. Man would go west in windwagons. No expense to buy horses or oxen to pull the wagons, no need to follow the river routes for water for the animals. Man would go west cheaper,

and he'd get there faster, sailing straight over the prairie on a forty-mile-an-hour wind.

Doc Taylor was one of those "show-me" Missouri men. He said, "What do you do when the wind doesn't blow?"

The beard billowed with laughter. "When *doesn't* the wind blow?" Anyway, Jones said, windwagons traveled so fast, they could afford a becalmed day now and then.

Howsomever, Ben Purdy and the others were Missouri men, too. So they set a test for Jones. He was to sail his windwagon over to Council Grove, Kansas, 150 miles away, and then come back. See how long it took him.

By then the wind was singing a whine in the shingles on the roof.

"Good stream flowing out there right now," said Jones. "Gentlemen, you're on!"

He hopped into his landship, let out the sail, and away he blew, beard pointed straight out in the wind for Council Grove, Kansas.

22

"Last we'll see of *that* crank," said one of the men, laughing.

Next day the wind died down, and the men settled on the bench in front of the stable to joke about the one-day wonder.

"Probably sitting out on the prairie, waiting for the air to move," Ben Purdy said with a chuckle.

"Or smashed up against a cottonwood tree," said another.

A week went by. No sign of Jones. They'd just about forgotten him, when along toward sundown the town dogs set up a bark. And there, rolling gently along on the breeze, came the windwagon. With Brown Beard at the helm.

He took in sail, pulled up to a stop, and jumped down with a paper in his hand. On it, written out fine, was a statement that Jones had been in Council Grove a few days before. It was signed by the town blacksmith.

"I know that smith, and he's an honest man!" Ben Purdy exclaimed. "Great shucks, Jones, you really did it!"

Whee, what a shout! The fellows gathered around Jones and slapped him on the back. Say, were those men excited! They formed a partnership right away. The Overland Navigation Company, they called it.

And the wagon they built! Big, I want to tell you! She was a mammoth.

The idea was that she'd be the master wagon for a fleet. She would haul a string of loaded wagons behind her, right across the the western prairie.

Jones and the men built their windwagon twenty-five feet long and seven feet wide. The wheels were twelve feet across, and the hubs alone were big as barrels. In fact, Jones got the bright idea that the hubs could hold the water supply the folks would need while crossing the dry prairie.

The men rigged her like a catboat, with mast well forward and only one sail. That mast was twenty feet high and carried the great cloth mainsail. The wagon box rose to the top of the wheels, twelve feet up, with a deck above that.

Boys, dogs, women with parasols—the whole town came to watch the building of the mighty wagon that would sail the plains like a ship. And at last she was done. There she stood, the ship of the plains, ready for the Glory Day, the day of her trial run.

It was a good day for the test. The wind had traveled over to eastern Missouri, and now it was backed up and ready to make the run for Kansas. The first breezes came frolicking by, flipping beards and bonnets. A fresh new day full of sun and wind, just right for a sail.

Windwagon Jones tied his beard down to his coat button with a string and hoisted himself up to the deck. "All aboard that's comin' aboard!" he shouted.

The partners climbed onto the deck, all except Doc Taylor. He said he'd come along behind on his mule. The fellows jeered at him, but Doc insisted. "I just might need this mule," he said.

The whole town turned out for the great event, the street fairly lined with folks. Hats waved and shouts went up.

"Hurrah for the windwagon!"

"She'll never move!"

Windwagon Jones let out sail, and every-
one cheered. But the breezes were still small,
and the wagon was monster-big. She didn't
move.

"Failure!"

"Get a horse!"

Ben Purdy signaled the youngsters gyrating around in the street. "Hi there, put a shoulder to it!"

A crew of boys pushed from behind, and Jones spread out all the sail. A gust came,

the wheels moved and— *hurrah, she's off!*
Slowly the great wagon began to creep
ahead. Around went the wheels, round and
around—the ship was under wind power!
Down the dusty street she trundled, picking
up speed, scattering boys and dogs to the
left and right.

"Hurrah! *Hurrah!*"

The fellows on board shouted and laughed it up to a hoot-n-holler. Windwagon Jones stood proud at the back, steering with the

wagon tongue. Out of Westport, onto the
prairie, sailed the ship of the plains. Doc
Taylor toed his mule and trotted after the
yelling crew.

And now the wind worked up to full blow, strong and steady, high wind for Kansas. Faster and faster flew the speedy

windwagon. Twenty-five miles an hour, thirty-five miles an hour. It was the fastest those men had moved in their lives.

"Whoo, boys!"

"Look at 'er whistle!"

They laughed and waved their hats at Doc Taylor, who was falling way behind on his mule.

About that time Windwagon Jones maybe should have taken in sail, for the wind was rising to a regular gale. But he didn't. He laughed and yelled with the rest as the wagon bounded over the ground, rising in the air when it hit the ditches.

"What'd I tell you? Didn't I tell you she'd sail?" Jones crowed like a brown-bearded banty. "Now watch this! Watch me run her against the wind!"

He put over his wagon-tongue helm. And the great ship of the plains obeyed. At first she came around in a grand sweep. But then something happened. The wind caught her sideways, turning the wagon and bringing her to a halt. Slowly the great wheels began to move again, but this time she started running in reverse.

Doc Taylor looked up and saw the whole wagonload coming at him lickety-cut, like to run over him. "Look out, you fools!" he cried. He turned his mule and galloped to get out of the way.

Then the windwagon began to go around in circles.

"Steering gear's locked!" yelled Jones. "Take in sail! Take in sail!"

The men quit laughing. All of a sudden this careening about in the high wind was fearsome. One fellow jumped overboard and hit the ground, rolling. Look out, boys! One after another, they all jumped off the wagon. And left Jones still yelling, "Take in sail!"

The mighty craft took bigger and bigger swoops until she was sailing around the prairie in mile-wide circles. The fellows could see Jones, good captain that he was, trying to furl the sail and fighting his beard, which had popped loose from the string in the gale.

Then, "There she goes!" Over the bank of Turkey Creek she flew, high against the sky. And dropped out of sight.

Doc Taylor first saw to the fellows scattered over the prairie, trotting his mule to each groaning man. But no one was really hurt, just bruises. So they picked themselves up and took off at a run for Turkey Creek to see what had happened.

There, fetched up at the bottom of the bank, all ker-smash at the bottom of the ditch, were the splintered remains of the ship of the plains. Windwagon Jones? Out from under the great canvas he crawled, pulling his beard down from his eyes so he could see.

"I told you to take in sail!" he said.

But that was the end of the story. That was the end of the Overland Navigation Company. Jones limped back to town and climbed into his first little windwagon. He put up just the right bit of cloth, and he sailed away.

They say in Westport, Missouri, that no one ever heard tell of him again. But stories grew up on the plains. Stories of a wagon that moved with a sail. The Indians told of a great bird with one white wing that flew the skies on a black, windy night. Could be. Set yourself out on the prairie and watch. You might be the one to see Windwagon Jones come sailing by on the western wind.

F
Ca   Calhoun, M.
       High Wind for Kansas.

DATE DUE			

GAYLORD M-2   PRINTED IN U.S.A.